ORCHARD BOOKS
Carmelite House
50 Victoria Embankment
London EC4Y 0DZ

First published in 2015 by Orchard Books

ISBN 978 1 40833 774 5

A CIP catalogue record for this book is available from the British Library.

2 4 6 8 10 9 7 5 3 1

Printed in Great Britain

MIX
Paper from
responsible sources
FSC® C104740

The paper and board used in this book are made from wood from responsible sources

Orchard Books is an imprint of Hachette Children's Group and published by the Watts
Publishing Group Limited, an Hachette UK company.

www.hachette.co.uk

Badly Drawn Beth

By Knife & Packer

ORCHARD

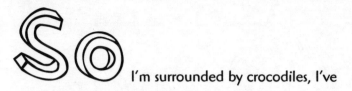 I'm surrounded by crocodiles, I've got a briefcase full of fish fingers, I'm wearing a swamp monster mask...

AND MISS PRIMULA IS ABOUT TO CALL MY PARENTS!!!

How did that happen? Let's go back to the beginning...

JANGLE!
JANGLE!
JANGLE!

My alarm clock RINGS...
and RINGS...
and RINGS...

The summer holidays are
officially OVER!
And that means one thing,
SCHOOL IS
STARTING.

YIKES!

I'm already in a sweat and I've only just woken up!

I should bounce out of bed, make myself breakfast

and high five the world. But today I feel tired,

and I want to know...

WHY?
WHY?
WHY???

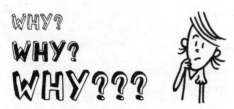

Why is it that every day of the school holidays

I got up at the crack of dawn? I felt as fresh as a daisy.

Fresh as a
daisy, tra
la tra la!

I was ready to rock. I could take on anything!

(Well, apart from maybe a

troll with really bad breath.)

But now that school is starting, when the alarm goes off I'm tired. I'm not even half awake...in fact, I'm so exhausted I want at least another three years of sleep! WHY?

I like school – it means friends, good times... But also

CLARISSA MUSGROVE.

I'll tell you more about her later – trust me, it's not good times.

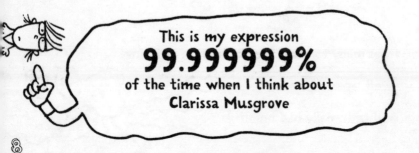

"LA LA LA GET DOWN, OH YEAH, BREAKFAST BOOGIE!!!"

But before I can tell you all about school, I need to explain the really annoying noise in the background. It's not a cat tuning up a broken violin, or someone scratching their fingernails on a board...

And now a piece in A Major...

A major disaster...

It's actually my dad. Singing. Who sings first thing in the morning? WHO???

(Answer: my dad.)

Because my dad is a MORNING PERSON.
Yes, he actually LIKES mornings – the earlier the
better – and he likes to sing and dance as he makes
breakfast.

Wicked!

snap!

Blocked-out area
so that you don't
have to look at
embarassing
dad dancing.

He occasionally stops singing and dancing to yell up the
stairs. "Get out of bed, Beth!" he screeches. Then he
starts singing again.

It's boogie-woogie
back to school...
YEAH!!!

Before I go downstairs, you've got to meet Scribbles.
He's my pet mouse. He nibbles stuff, sniffs stuff
and generally does a lot of mouse stuff.
But I'm SURE he gets up to more than that
when I'm not looking – like DJing...

...or running a clinic for
sick cockroaches.

One of the best things about
Scribbles is that my big sister
Mabel is terrified of him!

"BETH! Last warning!" shouts Dad. "Comb your hair and get down here! You don't want to be late for school, do you?"

Hmmm, Let me think about this for a minute...

Combing my hair is a bit of a daily battle. I brace myself, then quickly drag a comb through my hair. It's so tangly first thing in the morning there must be some **STRANGE** things in there...

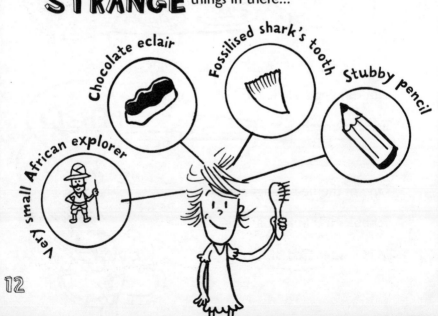

Chocolate eclair

Fossilised shark's tooth

Stubby pencil

Very small African explorer

Hair combed, clothes on, I'm now ready to face the

TERROR!

Because what I'm about to show you is something far

scarier than the darkest jungle...

...something far more terrifying than finding an alien in

your wash bag...

It's time for you to see breakfast – breakfast...with my family! Imagine a **chimps' tea party,**

throw in a couple of angry rhinos, oh yes, and a starving wildebeest and you're still not even close to the **chaos** of breakfast in my family...

I suppose you want to meet them? So here they are...

I might as well start with Mike Orsen, AKA **DAD** –
you've already heard him. He acts like he's about
twenty years younger than he is, which is super
embarrassing. He did some modelling in his youth,
mostly modelling cardigans

(which is even more embarrassing), and now he works
for a stationery company (Musgrove International Ltd.).

There's my Clarissa
Musgrove face again

Meet Penny Orsen, otherwise known as **MUM** – she's a teacher (at a different school, thankfully), which is cool because she can help with projects and homework, but is also not so cool because she's a...

STIKLER FOR RULES.

And here's my older sister **MABEL.** Mabel calls me

BADLY DRAWN BETH

because she once SPIED some self-portraits in my art

book. I think I look quite good in my drawings...

So Mabel is a grade A student,

grade A at sport and...

grade A at being **ANNOYING!**

Very
smug
smile

Finally, here's my younger brother **BERTIE**.

He drools a lot, spills stuff a lot – and that's about it.

BOING!

Bertie's favourite word

Bertie has a lot of energy!

So that's my family. Now you've met them you won't be surprised to see that today at breakfast Dad is trying to repair the juicer, while singing and dancing...

Mabel, who has probably already been up for six hours, is doing extra homework.

And Bertie is spilling Sugary Pops down my back...

Fortunately, Mum is just about holding things together and I get some breakfast.

"Pancakes – your favourite, Beth," says Mum, as she covers a huge stack of pancakes in yummy maple syrup. "Now, eat up – I've got to get ready for work...oh yes, and I've got to get the camera ready."

Because it's the first day of term, Mum insists on lining

us all up and taking a photo for Granny. I'm sure

Granny is sick of photos of us lined up looking either:

1. Embarrassed

2. Bored

3. Angry

(or sometimes all three)

FAKE SMILE ALERT!

Ooh a new set of snaps. How, er...lovely!

But she is just too polite to say so.

"You all look GORGEOUS," coos Mum.

All I can think about are the Sugary Pops that are stuck

down my back. When Mum finally gets the photo right

we can go to school.

I don't have to walk to school with my brother or sister. Bertie gets dropped off at nursery and my sister takes a bus to her school (and she probably does extra homework at the bus stop and on the bus).

If a bus goes at 20mph and stops at 31 stops how many cheese sandwiches are there in a lunchbox?

SNIFF
SNIFF
SNIFF

"Goodbye!" shouts Mum as I head off. "And be good!" I get to walk to school on my own – OK so it's just around the corner and I'm not really on my own. Everyday I join Cordy at the street corner. Cordy is my best friend ever, YOU ABSOLUTELY MUST MEET HER.

Real Name

CORDELIA MAVIS RUTLAND

Favourite Things

1. Night time

2. Black cats

3. Creepy buildings

4. The colour black

5. Strawberry milkshakes

6. Any TV show, book

or movie from The Dusk Light Sagas – werewolves are

sooooo cool (especially the star of the films:

Bobby Gothick).

Least Favourite Things

1. Ponies

2. Fairies

3. Unicorns

4. (And while we're at it, she says
that pink, frilly, fairy-tale princesses
who have been locked up in a tower
by an evil dragon, troll or stepmother
should be left there.)

Hobbies/Skills

Collecting moths
Able to dress in 12 shades of black

Catchphrase

"Woop, woop."
(Said when something ISN'T
really woop woop at all.)

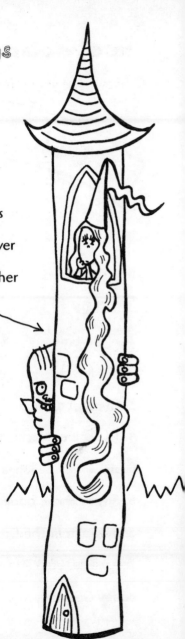

"Hi, Cordy," I say as we walk to school.
"How were your summer holidays?"

"Terrible. I was sent to live with a wicked ogre who eats
live puppy dogs and locked me in a cellar," says Cordy
in a quiet, scary voice.

I actually know she spent the summer with her aunt
Janine who lives near the sea. Her aunt Janine is
really nice, but Cordy likes to make things sound
scarier than they are.

"OK, so it wasn't all that bad," admits Cody. "We went swimming, had strawberry milkshakes, and you'll never guess what I saw at the cinema..."

"I don't know – haunted popcorn? A talking hotdog with legs?" I say.

"Don't be so silly, there's no such thing as haunted popcorn," laughs Cordy. "I saw a trailer for – wait for it – the new Dusk Light film!"

Cordy REALLY happy!

The Dusk Light Saga is AMAZING! It's all about teenage werewolves – there are books and magazines and lots of other stuff... The star of the films is **BOBBY GOTHICK** and he is just too cool for words.

OOOH!

Before we can talk more about the Dusk Light Saga we are interrupted by a big fancy car that honks noisily as it pulls up alongside us.

It's the
MUSGROVES!

I'm sorry, but it's time you met...

CLARISSA HORTENSE MUSGROVE

Favourite Things

1. Shopping

2. Shoes

3. Pink

4. Generally being

better than

everyone else

Least Favourite Things

1. The 'little people' who live in the 'little houses', especially me,

2. Cheap restaurants

3. Cheap clothes

4. Cheap anything

Hobbies/Skills

Has her very own pink **KIDDIE CREDIT CARD** and can buy every item in an average-sized shop in under thirty seconds.

CLARISSACARD

If she were stuck up a mountain, which three things would she want:

1. Her kiddie credit card

2. A sushi chef

3. A hot tub with a view

ME

Clarissa's mum has deliberately slowed down so Clarissa

can brag to us as she goes past...

Clarissa has a laugh a bit like an excited pony.

"Check out the wheels!" she screeches. "This car is blah, blah, turbo something, blah, blah fuel injection, blah, blah..."

I can't understand the car stuff so what I hear is:

Blah,
blah,
blah,
blah, 
BLAH,
BLAH,
BLAH, 
BLAH,
BLAH...

"Woop woop. Bor-ing," yawns Cordy in a loud voice.

"Let's go to school."

So there she is, Clarissa Musgrove. It's at times like this

I wish, I wish, I was a...

WITCH

But not any old witch – I wish I was a fully qualified

witch, taking my first steps into the world after leaving

Witch College...

TA DA!

spooky!

With my shiny new diploma tucked under my arm and a brand-new wart I would sort out Clarissa in style...

Firstly, I'd use a spell to turn their car into porridge – the really gloopy, lumpy kind that grannies make (well, my granny, anyway).

If Clarissa thinks being covered in porridge is bad it's just the start – because next I'd sprinkle her with super gross smelly cheese (the stinky, hard sort my parents have on their pasta – YUCK!)

Mummy!
I smell of Parmesan!

Then, and this is the REALLY fun bit, I'd summon up

a full cheesy moon and Scribbles (who has stowed away

in my school bag) would turn into...

Were-Mouse!

bounce!

A hideous, ravenous cheese-crazy mouse-monster who would eat the cheesy porridge car and then nibble Clarissa's toes in that tickly way that makes you giggle so much it hurts.

Stop it! No! Stop it! I've had enough! Please! Hee hee hee! Please stop it! Hee hee hee!

The cheese monster is going to get you!

I accidentally yell out loud.

"Cheese monster? What on EARTH are you talking

about?" scoffs Clarissa, shaking me out of my daydream.

"Oh, and by the way, your school bag should be in a

junk shop!"

(OK, so my bag is a bit old and moth-eaten, but only

Clarissa would point this out to the WHOLE world.)

So that's Clarissa — she's in my town, she's in my school, she's in my class, but that's not all... It actually gets WORSE!

As my dad works for *her* dad's company, they will be guests of honour at the annual family barbecue my parents are having soon. The Musgroves in MY house —

Just then we arrive at the school gates and I can forget about all that...for now.

We line up to go into class and everyone is there:

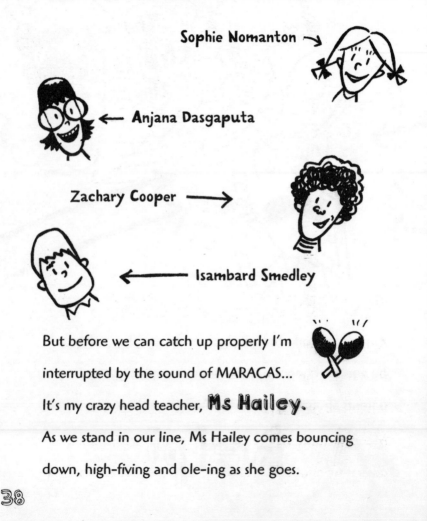

Sophie Nomanton →

← Anjana Dasgaputa

Zachary Cooper →

← Isambard Smedley

But before we can catch up properly I'm interrupted by the sound of MARACAS...

It's my crazy head teacher, **Ms Hailey.**

As we stand in our line, Ms Hailey comes bouncing down, high-fiving and ole-ing as she goes.

"¿QUÉ PASA, AMIGOS???"

Although everyone likes her she can be a bit over the top. Today she is dressed in a full Mexican outfit. What kind of a head teacher would be dressed in a Mexican outfit on the first day of term? Well, there are several types of head teacher that I have identified:

SOME HEAD TEACHERS THAT I HAVE IDENTIFIED:

The Trendy Head Teacher – they are cool and

down with the kids – yuck! If my dad

was a head teacher – no I don't even

want to go there...

The Old-School Head Teacher – they are quite

traditional, they like to dress in beige.

If they are a man they probably have

a beard.

The Really Old-School Head Teacher – they are like the

Victorians – SUPER STRICT!

Then there's Ms Hailey...

She is the kind of head teacher that loves any excuse to

dress up...and I mean any excuse.

And today, well today, it's because she went to Mexico

for her summer holidays!

When the school bell rings it's time to enter our BRAND-NEW classroom...to meet our BRAND-NEW teacher! We're about to charge into the classroom to grab the desks next to our friends when a scarily high-pitched, shrill voice cuts the air like a sharp knife through a birthday cake.

"There is a SEATING PLAN!" says the voice. "And my name is Miss Primula."

Miss Primula is my new form teacher for this year. As we quickly discover, Miss Primula (pronounced Prim-U-la) may look small and prim but she is NOT to be messed with. And THAT VOICE means you stop whatever you are doing and wait to be told what to do. "I have allocated everyone a place," barks Miss Primula, pointing to a plan on the board.

check out my startled look!

Sound waves of Miss Primula's voice

We all take our allocated seats and I sit at my desk...

THERE IS **GOOD** NEWS

I am next to Anju and opposite Zach.

ME

Anjana

Zach

AND...
THERE IS **BAD** NEWS

I'm *not* next to Cordy... BUT

fortunately there is no terrible news –

Clarissa is by the window quite far away.

"Now I want to find out about you..." Miss Primula says.

We now all have to say a bit about our summer holiday, which means STANDING UP IN FRONT OF THE WHOLE CLASS AND

SPEAKING.

I am now in a
COMPLETE
sweat!

We each have to talk for a whole minute. This is a little bit TERRIFYING. I imagine being struck by a weird, mystery illness which means I don't have to do it.

Miss! I seem to have a large mushroom growing out of my head!

But when I look down, my body is still human and there is no mushroom. Miss Primula tells us we also have to show a souvenir from our holiday.

"A letter went out at the end of last term," she reminds us. "I trust everyone brought something in..."

One by one everyone stands up to talk. As they do I start to PANIC...

There was a letter – a letter that my baby brother Bertie covered in strawberry jam. A letter I then forgot all about. First day of term, brand-new teacher and...

I HAVEN'T BROUGHT A SOUVENIR IN!

As the clock ticks, Anjana is first up...

I went on a beach holiday and the souvenir I brought in today is this piece of driftwood I found on the beach one evening. I think you'll find it looks a bit like Queen Elizabeth I.

Then it's Izzy. Izzy has brought in all the trophies and medals he won this summer.

I spent most of the summer at football camp.

Soon there's only two of us left to go –

Clarissa and ME...

"Well done, class – so far everyone has stuck to one minute exactly," says Miss Primula. "Clarissa, I can't wait to hear what you did..."

Unsurprisingly, a minute is not NEARLY enough time for Clarissa Musgrove (unless one Musgrove minute lasts for about four million seconds). And of course her holiday had to be...

THE BEST HOLIDAY IN THE WORLD EVER!

Blah
Blah
Blah
Blah

Doesn't she go on and on!

Clarissa is droning on and on. And on. And on. And on. And on. And on. And ON.

But for once I don't mind as I'm desperately trying to work out what I can show to the class. Meanwhile, in the background Clarissa is saying stuff about...

a cruise in a yacht...

shopping in the world's LARGEST shopping centre...

snorkelling in a tropical paradise...

snail wrestling...*

AND LOTS OF OTHER STUFF.

Take that!

Noooo!

*OK, I made up the bit about the snail wrestling.

But Miss Primula cuts her short just as Clarissa holds up her souvenir, an expensive looking handbag. I would have loved her to continue FOREVER because it's

ME NEXT.

"Clarissa, that sounds amazing, and your souvenir looks, um, very impressive," says Miss Primula.

Clarissa sits down and it's now my turn and the whole class is looking at me. But then, just in time, I have an idea... I don't have a souvenir, but I *do* have a story.

One night my mum and dad let me, my brother and sister to sleep in a tent in the back garden.

I look up and everyone seems interested (apart from
Clarissa, who is polishing her handbag). I take a deep
breath and continue.

I describe that night in the tent...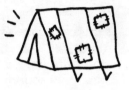
how my dad always says he is
'Mr Outdoors' – an expert in camping and
surviving in the wild (but on this trip he couldn't
stay out too long because of his 'bad knee').

How we ate sausages from the barbecue
(well, we tried but it was a bit too damp
so Mum cooked them inside).

It's getting
a bit warm
in here!

I THEN GET TO THE EXCITING BIT:

As night fell and we tried to get to sleep in our sleeping bags there was one small problem – MOSQUITOES, and lots of them! Bertie and Mabel quickly fled to the house. Only I survived the night!

OK, so that's what happened from MY point of view – I think the mosquitoes saw it more like this:

It's summer time and for the mosquitoes it's like the world is now a giant BUFFET...every human is a meal on legs, every child a tasty snack.

Meet Esmeralda and Stan, the mosquitoes that live in Beth's garden.

So when Beth, Mabel and Bertie settled into the tent for the night what Esmeralda and Stan saw was this:

And they didn't see two girls and their brother – what they saw was a large burger, a smaller burrito and a small but delicious ice cream pudding.

Unfortunately the burger and ice cream pudding very quickly decided to leave...

But the small burrito was DELICIOUS! Esmerelda and Stan just couldn't get enough!

"Basically, I got eaten alive," I say as quickly as I can, glancing at Miss Primula's clock.

"Ten seconds, Beth," warns Miss Primula. "You've got just enough time to show us your souvenir..."

I suddenly realise that I DO have a souvenir on me.

"Wait until you see these," I say as I pull down my sock.

"My collection of mosquito bites – live and in 3D!"

The class all GASP as they see my legs.

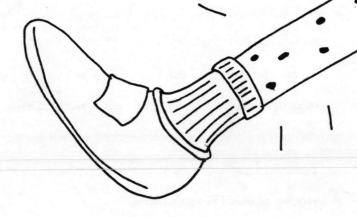

"Oh, that's TOO GROSS!" shrieks Clarissa, hiding behind her very expensive, very LARGE Italian leather handbag. "In fact, those look catching – I think Beth needs to be quarantined at ONCE!"

Those have got to be itchy!

"Er, congratulations, Beth," says Miss Primula, looking queasy. "Since you are obviously good with animals... YOU can be the first to look after the new class pet. Just for a few weeks, and don't worry – you're going to get on just fine."

There is **HUGE** excitement

in the room, a class pet – what can it be?

"Say hello to Edgar!" Miss Primula fetches a glass box

from underneath her desk.

"He's a bearded dragon! Like most pet reptiles, Edgar lives in a VIVARIUM."

"Ha ha *neigh* ha!" jeers Clarissa as she looks at me.

"It's a MONSTER! Good luck with THAT!"

Clarissa's
jeering face

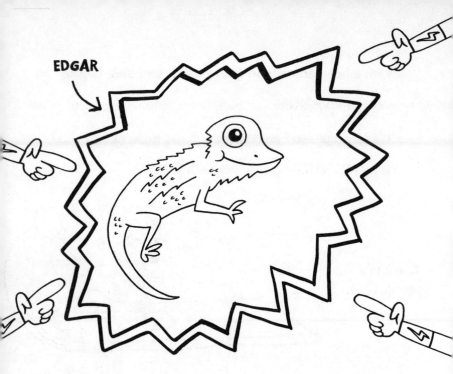

EDGAR

I don't know what to say – I've never looked after a
lizard before.

"I'll give you some lizard food and instructions – you'll
be fine, Beth," says Miss Primula, before addressing the
whole class. "This term's theme is NATURE. In fact,
there will be a very exciting guest at assembly soon, but
I'm not giving the surprise away..."

At the end of the school day I need a lift from Mum to get Edgar and his vivarium back home. Mum is not too sure about this new house guest.

The first day of term is over officially OVER...
GREAT BIG PHEW!

I've got to settle Edgar into his new home – MY ROOM! And Scribbles does NOT look impressed.

I am not happy about this!

C'mon, Scribbles – think about it – reptiles and rodents, living together in perfect harmony!

Oh, please!

"Beth, dinner time!" shouts Mum.

When I go downstairs I like to think that Edgar and Scribbles are having a lovely happy time together up in my room...

Playing ping-pong...

Discussing world politics...

Or maybe singing peace songs...

But to be honest as long as they're not fighting I'll be happy.

At school a few days later there is SPECIAL ASSEMBLY and as you can imagine there is a lot of excitement in the playground.

"I think Miss Primula has gone over to the Dark Side," says Cordy, frowning. "Ms Hailey has called this assembly to see if any of the other teachers have become vampires..."

"I think it may be to do with the building site behind the main hall," says Zachary Cooper.

This sounds more likely, even though it's a lot more BORING than Cordy's theory.

"Maybe there's going to be a new sports competition!" gasps Izzy Smedley, who is football mad.

There is a BUZZ of excitement as we all sit in rows with our classes when Ms Hailey comes bouncing into the hall – wearing KHAKI and an EXPLORER'S HAT.

Hellooooooooo and welcome to assembly!

As she makes some 'important announcements' about stuff like where to store PE kit and punctuality for school clubs, my mind starts to wander...

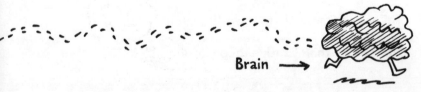

Brain →

Ms Hailey dressing up like a Victorian explorer – it all makes sense...

She probably keeps a
WATER BUFFALO in
her office — that's why very
few people ever go in there...

and there's almost certainly a **PYTHON** in the glove
compartment of her car — which is why she very rarely
offers anyone a lift...

and when she goes home she probably keeps a
WARTHOG in her bathroom!

I'm shaken out of my daydream as Ms Hailey says she has

a special guest. In fact, she has had guests before...

A fire-eater friend of

hers burnt down part

of the staff room...

 All I did was burp!

A DJ she was at college with blew the

school sound system...

And her next door

neighbour who was a

hairdresser ended up giving the

school janitor (Reginald Mavers)

a disastrous haircut...

 I do not approve of the Mohican as a hairstyle!

"Today's guest has been a wildlife pioneer for years,"

declares Ms Hailey. "And he has something very exciting

to tell you all!"

During Ms Hailey's talk, several large boxes have been placed behind her. There are various scratchings and snufflings coming from the boxes – this is getting EXCITING! There's a lot of feverish whispering amongst our class as we guess what the animals might be. Finally the stage is ready...

"Please welcome Giles Goddard!" booms Ms Hailey. "Safari park owner and **DANGEROUS-WILDLIFE HANDLER!**"

GILES GODDARD, the owner of Goddard's World of Wonderbeasts – the town's super exciting safari park, here, in our school?

This is A-MA-ZING. The whole school goes

Giles Goddard arrives on stage. Not only that, but he has brought some animals with him...

Watchya, wildlife watchers!*

*That's his catchphrase!

Mr Goddard dramatically sweeps around the stage uncovering the boxes that have been placed there. I can't believe we are about to see terrifying wild creatures in our school!

But with each box he opens the crowd gets a

little less excited.

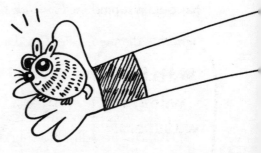

"Observe the Chinese

dwarf hamster!"

"And lo – the

Peruvian guinea pig!"

Cousins!

There is a loud **GROAN** from the audience.

"OK, OK, I'm sorry, it's HEALTH AND SAFETY,"

mumbles Mr Goddard apologetically. "These are not the

'top of the food chain' beasts of my wildlife park. You

just can't bring lions and tigers in to schools any more.

But there is ONE FINAL BOX..."

Finally he stands by the last box...SURELY this has got to contain something REALLY EXCITING. The lights are dimmed, Giles Goddard holds a torch under his chin for dramatic effect and drops his voice...

"BEHOLD!" he yells, throwing open the box. But it's EMPTY. "Jemima – she has broken loose!" barks the wildlife tycoon. "It's an EMERGENCY!"

There is a brief panic in the hall as we all check over our shoulders, under our feet and down our jumpers for signs of the beast...

Should I call the police?

Or the fire brigade?

Knees knocking

"What is Jemima?" screeches Ms Hailey, standing on a chair. "A vicious brute who needs to be treated with extreme caution?"

"She is a GIANT African land snail," explains Mr Goddard, "follow the slime trail!" Jemima is quickly located on Mr Furble (the gym teacher's) packed lunch.

"We are holding a COMPETITION," announces Giles

Goddard, when everyone's calmed down. "Schools across

the country are to CRAFT their own menagerie

of MODEL animals. You can use any materials you like.

But your most important tool must be – your

imaginations!"

"And the prize?" interrupts Ms Hailey.

"The best overall class, with the most variety and most interesting use of materials, will win itself a free trip to my safari park! And trust me – the animals there are

SPECTACULAR..."

SPECTACULAR?
I can balance cheese on my nose!

The crowd claps, and I clap too. In fact, I liked most of what he just said... I liked the bit about a trip to his safari park (I've never been), I liked the bit about a competition...

But there's a bit I didn't like. The bit I didn't like was...

The bit about  CRAFT.

I have a bit of a 'tricky' relationship with arts and crafts.
Here are just a couple of my most recent ARTS AND
CRAFTS DISASTERS:

My Aztec temple looked more like
an archaeological ruin after the
loo roll tubes and a dozen lolly sticks collapsed.

And my model rainforest looked like
a tornado had blown through and it
had to be declared a cardboard
cut-out disaster zone.

I think you get the idea.

Edgar has been staying with me for a couple of weeks and it's gone quite well. As long as you feed him and give him water he really is no trouble at all.

Well, actually the food he eats is a bit – actually **SERIOUSLY** – icky, but I'll tell you about that later...

CHOMP! CHOMP!

As Edgar tucks into his lunch the doorbell RINGS – it's Cordy.

BEST FRIEND!

She has come over so we can build our arts and crafts

animals together. Unfortunately Cordy is even WORSE

at arts and crafts than I am.

"It's a **TOTAL DISASTER!**" groans Cordy as she

slumps on my bed.

"I thought you were bringing the vampire bat

you were making from old shoes?" I say.

"I have. It's in my bag," replies Cordy, before she spots

something. "Hey, what's that?"

She points at my school bag. My old school bag is now

in such a bad state that it's become seriously

EMBARRASSING.

But I distract her by grabbing the plastic bag she has

brought with her.

I tip up the bag and out falls

ONE BLACK PLIMSOLL. It doesn't even

have wings stuck on it yet.

Mmm!
Cheesy!

"It still needs a little bit of work,"

I observe tactfully.

"A BIT? IT NEEDS ABOUT ONE

HUNDRED YEARS OF WORK,"

moans Cordy. "My parents are

no help at ALL!"

Most people get their parents to do all the art and craft stuff for them, but our parents are USELESS.

"What about your parrot?" asks Cordy

parrot??

I'm making a model of Granny's parrot in papier-mâché. At the moment I have a papier-mâché sculpture shaped a bit like a pyramid.

"We need help," declares Cordy. We have a quick go at building our animals but soon decide that arts and crafts STILL aren't our thing and that instead we need to do something really important...

something vital, in fact. Because we need to...

HANG OUT!

This involves chatting, plotting and more chatting.

"Remember the NEW DUSK LIGHT film I saw the trailer for on holiday?" says Cordy, her eyes lighting up. "Well, it's showing in the local cinema! But there's more..."

"MORE? You say there is... MORE!?!" I gasp.

"Well, there IS. Much, much MORE!" continues Cordy. "There are rumours of a PERSONAL APPEARANCE AT THE LOCAL CINEMA BY BOBBY GOTHICK!"

If you haven't read the books, you need a super-quick guide to the Dusk Light Saga in...

Beth's super-quick guide to the Dusk Light Saga

In an invented town somewhere in America a group of regular kids are doing regular things in a regular school...

There's Brad Laverne (swoon) – he 'plays ball' – and there's his best friend Kim Mangiani, she's a cheerleader. Then a mysterious new boy comes to school, DeShaun Matrice (played by Bobby Gothick in the movies – DOUBLE SWOON!).

Except they aren't that regular – in fact (and this is the twist), they AREN'T REGULAR AT ALL.

Because they are actually teenage WEREWOLVES!

So when there is a full moon they have to slip out of their all-American houses and do werewolf things.

Can Brad and Kim still be best friends when they are covered in FUR? Can love blossom when DeShaun's TEETH are that SHARP?

And can you drink out of a dog bowl without making a huge MESS?

"I got TWO promotional masks from the latest Dusk Light magazine," says a super-excited Cordy, handing me a mask. "I carry mine about with me ALL THE TIME. As my best friend YOU can have the spare one..."

"THANKS, CORDY! So the next Dusk Light film has a swamp monster?" I gasp in awe, putting on the mask.

Grrrrrr!

We decide it would be really funny to sneak up on my parents wearing our masks. They are DEEP in concentration.

My dad is scrubbing bits off the barbecue

and my mum is polishing cutlery...

It's easy to tell when my parents are REALLY concentrating – my mum's mouth hangs open and my dad sticks his tongue out.

"OK, here goes!" I whisper to Cordy.

We both jump out in front of my parents –

with BEASTLY SHRIEKS

and **MONSTER SHOUTS!**

Awooga!

Ugunga!

Rarrr!

Grawr!

Rarrr!

Grawr!

AND...nothing.

Mum mutters something like, "Ooh, that's nice, dear,"

but doesn't even look up from what she's doing. In fact,

there is full-blown panic downstairs. My parents are a

blur of preparation...

"What's up with them?" says Cordy. "Have they been changed into zombies?"

And that's when it comes back to me...

"Worse!" I reply. "The Annual Family Barbecue is fast approaching! Lots of guests – including... The Musgroves."

Woop, woop. What's the big deal?

Oh dear!

It's time to explain why OUR barbecue involves VIP guests like no other...

THE MUSGROVES (yes, those Musgroves)

A brief history of my family (the Orsens) and the Musgroves

Many, many years ago my parents went to the same school as the Musgroves – of course they weren't 'the Musgroves' then, they were plain Donny and Muriel...and my parents weren't 'the Orsens' – they were Mike and Penny.

Apparently, back then Donny and Muriel were quite nice, in fact, they used to be best friends with my parents...

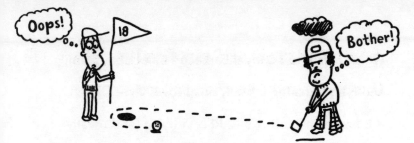

But then Donny Musgrove lost to my dad at golf – and
Dad ended up WORKING for their family company:
Musgrove International Ltd...

Meanwhile Muriel Musgrove, who
used to be my mum's best friend,
won the local beauty contest. She
thought she was going to become
an INTERNATIONAL star and

ditched all her local friends, including my mum...

And when that didn't
work out she married Donny
and they've been THE
MUSGROVES ever since...

Which means our annual barbecue is not about family and friends sharing a lovely meal together – OH NO... it is basically about MY PARENTS trying (and usually FAILING) to impress the Musgroves.

"Ah, Beth, Cordy," says Mum, looking up from the cutlery. "There are LOADS of jobs you could do..."

"Who here wants to do some SCRUBBING?" adds Dad.

We quickly decide that our arts and crafts projects are much more important and we escape.

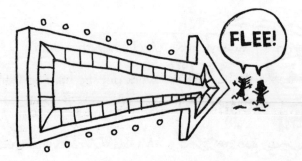

The next morning and my school bag is really starting to give me some PROBLEMS (or, as my dad would say: "PROBLEMOS"). It is now officially beyond repair.

But my dad 'comes to the rescue'.

SUPERDAD!

"Have this," he says. And he hands me a bag that is so **HORRENDOUS** I don't even want to show it to you.

my poor old bag!

That day at school arts and crafts is ALL THAT EVERYONE IS TALKING ABOUT

Anjana Dasgaputa is NATURALLY GOOD at art (which feels like cheating) and she is making a family of baboons out of cereal packets...

Sophie Normanton

Anjana Dasgaputa

Sophie Normanton's parents are both ART TEACHERS so of course she is getting loads of help... Her matchstick stick insects sound awesome!

We're all having a really good chat when Clarissa swaggers across.

I imagine she has an entire team of engineers from her dad's firm designing her animal. In fact, I wouldn't be surprised if she had a vast hangar where her animal is being built by huge teams of ROBOTS!

She is just about to open her mouth when luckily the school bell rings.

We are soon in class and Miss Primula has to use THAT VOICE to quieten us down.

"LISTEN UP," she snaps. "I have a really exciting announcement." She smiles. "Now as you know there has been some building work at the back of the school... Well we are going to be the first class to visit this new area."

There have been rumours about what's been happening in there – and counter rumours.

I think it's a worm farm!

But the best guesses I have at the moment are:

1. It's a secret bunker where Ms Hailey will store her outfits

2. It's the nerve centre of an international spying organisation with the head spy being school janitor Reginald Mavers

The name's Mavers. Reginald Mavers. And I have a license to clean toilets...

But I never would have guessed it was...

"A POND!" Miss Primula grins triumphantly as we arrive at the newly unveiled site. "That's right, the school has built its very own pond!"

Miss Primula hopes we will see some wildlife to help inspire our models.

The trouble with ponds is that quite often there isn't
much going on.

"All I can see is water," grumbles Zachary Cooper.

"And I can see weeds," adds Izzy Smedley.

But that's it – apart from that a big, fat

NOTHING.

But then I spot it – THE CREATURE – winding through
the water. It's slithery, it's a bit scary and it's alive...

"**SNAKE!**" I shout. "It's a...

"A chocolate wrapper," says Miss Primula,
fishing the wrapper out with a net.

But as she looks down there's a loud SPLASH. Her glasses have fallen in!

"They're sinking!" she squeals.
"Help – I can't see!"

I'm convinced I see a flash of green – there is wildlife in the pond after all.

Maybe a NEWT HAS GRABBED THE GLASSES...

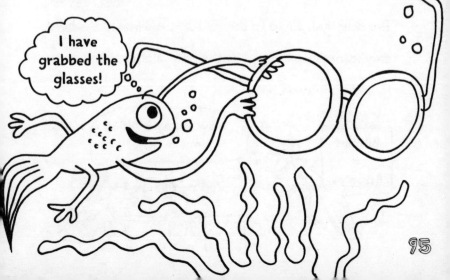

I have grabbed the glasses!

And not just any old newt...maybe there's a **NEWT KINGDOM** under the glassy surface of the school pond...

Deep under the water, adult newts go about their daily business. They commute to work in Newt City...

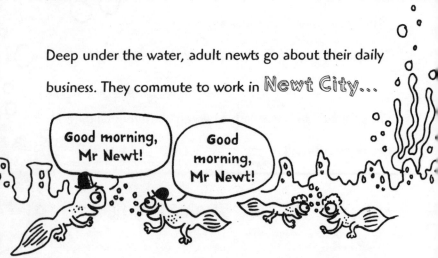

Good morning, Mr Newt!

Good morning, Mr Newt!

The newt kids all go to the Newt School – where they learn newt things, like the newt alphabet and how to add up in newt.

Bibbles + Bubbles

How many bibbles in a bubble?

And at the heart of the Newt Kingdom is the Newt
Palace – a magnificent structure built from
pebbles and bits of pond debris.

In the centre of this palace is the throne room – heavily
guarded by vicious attack-frogs and angry tadpoles...

And if you could have a look through the door into
the most secret and private place in the whole Newt
Kingdom you would see the Newt King and the Newt
Queen – sitting on a beautiful and unique throne, a
throne made...from Miss Primula's glasses!

"Hey, my teacher wants her glasses back, you slimy
newts!" I shout.

It's time for me to change into SARDINE-GIRL.
Half girl, half sardine, all underwater action hero!

When I am SARDINE-GIRL
I can breathe underwater!

"BETH! WHAT DO YOU THINK YOU'RE DOING!"
shouts Miss Primula in her MOST SCARY VOICE.

My teacher has woken me up from my daydream – just
when I was about to jump into the pond!

Just then the school janitor arrives.

"You're my hero, Mr Mavers," gushes Miss Primula. The
school janitor rolls up his sleeves.

"It's mucky work, but someone's got to do it," he says,
fishing out various gross bits of weed and slimy things.
Eventually he finds the glasses.

There you go, Miss Primula.

Oh, Mr Mavers, you're quite fearless!

Later, I'm in the playground about to head home.

Cordy and I are CHATTING as usual.

"The next time I see that much water I hope it's the
LAKE in the Dusk Light Movie," declares Cordy.

"There was almost a snake there," I mumble.

But Cordy suddenly stops talking and her eyes pop out
of her head – she has seen something AWFUL!

Oh no! It's my NEW SCHOOL BAG. I had hoped

people wouldn't notice it because it's, well, let's face it,

pretty horrendous...

"Your bag, it's, it's..." stutters Cordy in disbelief.

"It's a briefcase," I say as I
reluctantly hold up my new
bag for closer inspection.
It is indeed a briefcase.

"How did you end up with a bag like that?" asks Cordy.
So I have to tell her the whole story...

How I'd loved my old bag – how when I saw it all lonely in a shop I took it in and gave it a home.

How we had been through good times and bad. How it had always been there for me, how it never complained about being stuffed with books and stinky gym kit (SNIFF!).

But how finally my beloved old bag had been patched up once too often, so one day (HUGE **DOUBLE SNIFF!**) it had to be retired.

"That's *almost* sad," sighs Cordy, unsympathetically. "But it's a SCHOOL BAG we're talking about here. So where did you get the new bag?"

I now explain where the new case came from – how 'LUCKILY' my dad stepped in. Because 'FORTUNATELY' thanks to his job at Musgrove International he had ended up with a lot of (slightly faulty) briefcases.

This executive model is fan-tas-tic!

"So it's on LOAN from my dad." I make it clear. "As soon as we go to the shops I'll be getting a new one."

The trouble is there are just so many bags to choose from.

BETH'S GUIDE to school bags

1. The Star Bag.

This is likely to go out of
fashion. Who has heard of
boy band The Chiselled
Chaps? Exactly. Or child
acting sensation Macee
MacMurphy? No, didn't think so.

2. The Cute
Character Bag.

This can be too cheesy.
I mean, Mr Pumpkin-Head,
really? Talking Pumpkins are
not cute!

3. The Leather Bag.

These are squeaky, smelly and will go out of fashion even faster than a Chiselled Chaps record or Macee MacMurphy's *My Buddy is a Baboon* movie.

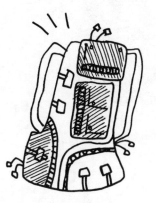

4. The Technical Outdoor Bag.

Fine if you're going trekking or planning to climb a mountain, but for school use? Forget it.

Are all those zips and toggles really necessary?!

Where's the cheese pocket?

When I get home I immediately get to work persuading Dad to take me to the shopping centre to buy a new bag.

But something is not quite right. In fact something is definitely **WRONG**.

Because he agrees...right away!

"Great idea," chirps Dad as he jumps out of his chair, puts on his driving cardigan (he has Chunky Knit cardigans for most activities) and bounces towards the front door.

Chunky driving cardigan made out of some weird fluffy wool

Car keys

As soon as we get in the car Dad puts the car stereo on **AT MAX VOLUME**. My dad insists on playing what he calls 'happy driving tunes'.

"This music really is groo-vy," he hums, clearing his throat. I know what comes next – singing.

And if the choice of music isn't bad enough, the sound system on our car seems to have a special volume setting. There is loud, **really loud**, and then there is **happy driving tunes** loud...a volume so loud that it can affect the flight of birds, a volume so loud that moles deep underground can't play chess for the noise.

And when my dad sings along, it's so loud I bet they can even hear it in space!

But there is worse to come. Because rather than head to the shopping centre, Dad has to make a detour.

"Is that the time?" he gasps,

looking at his watch.

"I've got to make

AN **EMERGENCY** STOP!"

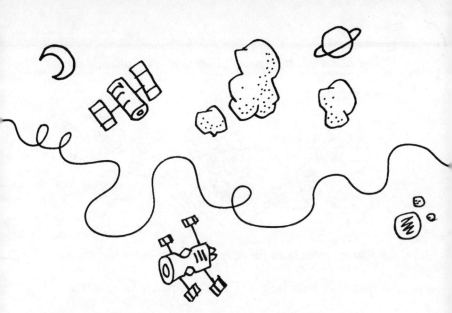

Only my dad would need to make an EMERGENCY

STOP at a FISHMONGERS.

"It's for the barbecue," he explains.

This year is going to be different. The key this year is TOP QUALITY FOOD...

Every year my dad has a theory on how this barbecue will be different and better.

And this year it is...fish.

"This place is fish heaven," Dad says as he disappears into the shop.

A few minutes later he reappears with more fish than I have ever seen before. There's so much fish that we can't fit it all in the car! We have to stuff fish fillets in the boot and fish pies in the glove compartment. Dad even has to cram his BRIEFCASE full of posh fish fingers!

"The Musgroves are going to LOVE THIS STUFF!"

This all takes AGES and the shopping centre is now SHUT! So no new bag for me.

The next day we're walking into school. I'm trying

to keep my briefcase hidden as best I can when I hear

THAT LAUGH.

It's Clarissa. I knew she would spot it eventually. But

before I can reply I notice something strange about

Clarissa – she's...WALKING!

It turns out the family car is being repaired and now she has to walk with us – the 'little people' who live in the 'little houses'!

"This is soooo sweet," she says. "Walking! It's really cute. Shame the air is so disgusting down here. That's why we always drive with the air-con on max..."

You see, in the town where I live the BIG houses are all at the top of the hill. In fact sometimes I wish I could turn into a **GIANT.**

The kind of giant with
SUPER-BAD BREATH...

And feet that smelled of a
thousand rotting EGGS...

Then I could show you the BIG HOUSES and when I
got to Clarissa's house I would breath through her
bedroom window and my breath
would MELT all her stuff...

I would then have a paddle in her king-size
swimming pool and my stinking giant feet
would turn the water green and toxic...

And finally I would sit
my wobbly giant
bottom on her super
smug PONY – not quite
long enough to turn it
into pony pizza...

Did someone
say pizza?!?

Luckily, right now I don't even need to be a giant because Clarissa, out of her big fancy car and having to WALK like the rest of us, is not feeling too pleased with herself. This is **BRILLIANT!**

But unfortunately I can't be too smug:

@. Because I have a ridiculous school bag and

b. Because the family barbecue is coming up and my mum made me PROMISE to be nice to Clarissa as she thinks we are going to be 'the best of friends'.*

*I don't think even **Mum** believes that is really going to happen.

As we approach school, something MUCH MORE IMPORTANT than Clarissa's blabbering GRABS OUR ATTENTION.

It's Cordy who sees it first – then me...and it's

The new Dusk Light film poster!

"Not long now!" gasps Cordy. "I can hardly wait..."

The school day speeds by as we talk about the film.

The next day is Saturday, but it starts TERRIBLY!
Scribbles has gone missing!

I have to turn my whole room over and I finally

find him in what my mum calls 'the pile of

rubbish' in the corner of my room (or as

I call it: MY PARROT MODEL-MAKING ZONE).

He had accidentally got stuck under my masterpiece!

I finally get him unstuck when my dad calls up the stairs.

"It's time to go to Mega Pet World," Dad bellows.

Edgar has run out of food, and the only place we can get his special lizard grub is the out of town pet depot.

Gathering everyone to get in the car is quite a job and it takes Mum and Dad every ounce of their energy to load us up.

Dad puts on the happy driving tunes, the rest of us block our ears, and we're off...

Before long we have reached our destination:

Happy shiny mornings!

MEGA PET WORLD

Stuff you need to know about Mega Pet World:

1. It sells pets, food for pets, things for pets

2. Its so huge it's **MEGA**

3. Er, that's all

This place is a pet-lovers' paradise and I can't wait to get

inside...

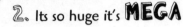

MEGA PET WORLD!

Mabel doesn't want to leave the car (so she can keep reading her SCIENCE BOOK) but me and Bertie are desperate to explore.

I check out the fish tanks...

Hope they don't know about the BBQ...

The dog grooming area...

And of course the lizard food – which I think I already mentioned is quite ICKY!

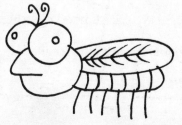

But then a loud PUBLIC ADDRESS ANNOUNCEMENT booms through the store – there is going to be a demonstration on how to look after reptiles at home. Perfect!

This is GREAT! A lady gives us lots of tips on how to look after all kinds of reptiles...

Reptile Care Tips

1. Make sure your lizard is healthy by checking their skin, eyes and nose – a runny nose is a sign of sickness. Edgar seems well but I will remember to check.

2. Take your lizard out regularly: lizards need exercise. Mabel is not going to like that one.

3. They don't like sudden movements, but tickling them under the chin can calm them down – I make a mental note in case Edgar ever goes MAD.

4. They like fresh and LIVE* food. Time to shop!
*See, I told you it was ICKY!

As soon as we have bought the LIVE crickets we can head home. My mum and dad have made me PROMISE to keep them in their container – but of course I can't resist playing a trick on my sister...

On Sunday it's **GRANNY DAY!**

I love visiting Granny. For starters,

she has the best cakes...

She has funny stories (mostly about Mum)...

> **And then your mum ate a handful of bird seed!**

> Please, Mum!

She has a huge collection of EMBARRASSING

photos, mostly of Mum, but some of Mum and Dad

(and some of me too, but I won't be showing you any

of those)...

Mum aged three!

Younger Dad looking cheesy!

But best of all she has a pet parrot called Otto. Mabel, of course, HATES Otto, but then Otto doesn't like her either (most animals don't).

"Hello, me darlings!" beams Granny.
"Come on in...I've been baking!"

As soon as we get to Granny's we all sit down for CAKE. Now, you need to know some important stuff about Granny's cakes. We all like cakes, right? (Well, apart from Mabel but I think we have established she is WEIRD.)

My granny's cakes are more than just cakes — they are covered in goodies, chocolaty things and other all-round bits of YUMMINESS. This is beyond icing, this is her special recipe stuff.

Icing

Strawberries

Cream

Cherries

Jam

Fruity bit

More cream and more jam

Meringue "swirls"

Nearly done, me dears!

Because her recipes are

TOP SECRET

no one knows how she makes

them — although I'm

pretty sure it involves a

ladder and

a spoon the size

of an OAR...

Granny cake-mix vat!

As we all tuck into the cake, Granny launches into a
SUPER EMBARRASSING story about my mum
when she was seven...

Apparently Mum's regular hairdresser was off sick and so
her younger sister stood in – but she had NEVER CUT
HAIR BEFORE. Not only that, but she had a broken
wrist so her arm was in a sling... (Well, that's what it
looks like from the way Mum's hair turned out!)

Granny holds up a picture and we all get to see the
HAIRSTYLE CALAMITY.

After we have eaten tea we move though to the
LOUNGE. This is my second favourite part of a visit to
Granny's but everyone else dreads it. Because in her
lounge we get to see Granny's pet parrot, Otto.

My mum, Dad and
Mabel and Bertie are all
convinced that Otto is
EVIL. I accept he is
quite badly behaved –
in fact, there are times he
is so badly behaved he
seems like an evil genius.

Like the time he
pecked my dad's
favourite Party Cardigan so much all that
was left was a handful of wool.

Or the time my mum was taking an important work call

and he kept screeching, "Nutty biscuits!"

It was quite hard for Mum to explain to her boss what

nutty biscuits were.

Today is no different and Otto is soon shouting, "FRUITY PANCAKES!" at Dad and pecking at Mabel's science book (that she brought because it's a 'fun read').

Otto has always liked me and I manage to calm him down. Which is good, because I have a big favour to ask Granny. There is something I need – something only Granny (well, Otto, really) can provide...

FEATHERS.

"It's no trouble, dearie," Granny says. "Otto is always shedding. Sometimes I find that me trifle is full of feathers!"

"FLUFFY TRIFLES!"

squawks Otto from the other room, as he attacks my mum's hair. Otto never seems to stay on his perch but instead flaps from sofa to sofa – which explains why Mabel always sits on the floor at Granny's.

Back home I feed Edgar (MEGA ICK), then it's time to work! I put the final touches to my parrot model, using the real feathers Granny kindly gave me.

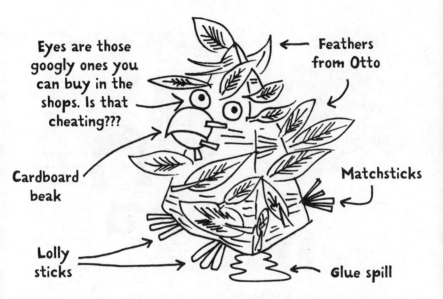

Eyes are those googly ones you can buy in the shops. Is that cheating???

Feathers from Otto

Cardboard beak

Matchsticks

Lolly sticks

Glue spill

But in all the making, taping and glueing of my model parrot I suddenly realise there is one thing I have completely forgotten about – getting a new school bag!

Looks like another week of the briefcase!

When I get to school the next day everyone seems to be carrying a model for the competition. In fact it's just like an arts and crafts day.

I have brought my parrot, Cordy has brought her bat.

Oh, Cordy!

I really don't do craft things.

One of the **BIG PROBLEMS** with arts and craft days is the PARENTS. For some reason parents seem to feel the need to get involved and they are EVERYWHERE...

There are fussing parents, there are bragging parents and there are competitive parents...

Beth's Guide to Parents on Arts and Craft Days:

1. The Art Expert

He or she went to art school and has DONE ALL THE WORK.

If you've studied art in Venice you can do anything with an egg box, darling.

2. The Wannabe Art Expert

They THINK they are good at art but actually their stuff is rubbish (although it doesn't stop them commenting on everyone else's).

Call that a tortoise?

3. The OK-At-Art-But-Was -Up-All-Night Parent

They have bags under their eyes and often drop the artwork on the way to school.

It fell in a puddle!

Fortunately, Ms Hailey doesn't take kindly to her playground being invaded and she is soon shooing parents out.

"That's it, everyone out!" she barks. "Yes, that includes you, Mrs Abercrombie. And, I'm sure you are very proud of your daughter's model, but you're going to have to leave, Mr Patel..."

Sanjita Patel and her amazing elephant!

Despite the fact that
Ms Hailey is dressed as a
PENGUIN, none of the
parents hang around to
argue with her.

But even Ms Hailey is
stopped in her tracks by a loud siren...

BEEP BEEP BEEP PARP PARP

It's the sound of a
large lorry reversing in
front of the school. It's
a Musgrove
International van,
and inside is Clarissa
and her creation.

"Now, come along, men," says Clarissa bossily, as she
oversees the delivery of HER ANIMAL - a full-size
giraffe!

Ms Hailey
waddles across.
"Ooh, well done,
Miss Musgrove,"
she coos. "I think this
magnificent specimen is going
to have to grace the school
stage!"

When we finally make it into
class, Miss Primula helps us place
all the animals in position. Each
class has its own space in the hall,
and the best ones are on the stage.

Clarissa's giraffe looms over all the others, looking down on them snootily.

"Well, it's an, er, mixed bag, but I feel quite good about this," says Miss Primula as she puts the last animal in position.

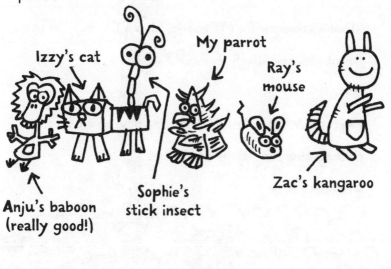

Izzy's cat

My parrot

Ray's mouse

Anju's baboon (really good!)

Sophie's stick insect

Zac's kangaroo

"Be careful, Miss Primula," Cordy gasps, as one of her bat's wings wobbles dangerously.

"The judges will be coming next week," Miss Primula tells us.

I hope the models last that long – some of them seem to be falling apart already!

"Thank goodness for MY giraffe," hisses Clarissa. "Your parrot looks positively SCARY..."

I wish my MODEL PARROT would come to life and peck Clarissa repeatedly on the head, like a woodpecker.

It's another weekend and arts and craft animals,

competitions and Clarissa being pecked by model

parrots are all forgotten about because it's

SATURDAY...

BUT NOT ANY OLD SATURDAY...

BECAUSE IT'S THE DAY OF...

THE BARBECUE

(Today does not feel like it's going to be a good day.)

My parents have turned into raving monsters. It's like they are evil barbecue robots, destroying anything in their path that might get in the way of their precious barbecue.

I need a weekend away from my family!

"Must wear right cardigan," says my dad in his robo voice. "MUST IMPRESS MR MUSGROVE."

Must prepare sausages!

Must talk about golf!

As I mentioned, my dad used to be a cardigan model and he has narrowed the choice of cardigan down to three:

Meanwhile Mum is waging war – on her own hair!

"NEED BIGGER HAIR!" she crackles in her robo voice. "Mrs Musgrove will only like me if I have GREAT HAIR!"

As I said before, Mrs Musgrove was once the local beauty queen because of her legendary hair. Which may explain why my mum seems to get competitive about her hair when Mrs Musgrove is visiting.

143

In amongst all this madness I would happily hide in my bedroom, out of the way. I could hang out with Edgar and Scribbles.

We could start a band, a circus, or, wait for it, a detective agency – specialising in INSECT CRIMES...

But us kids are expected to be...

And when Mum's hair can get no bigger and when Dad has picked his cardigan (The Barbecue Boss, if you're interested), then the attention is turned on US!

As if things weren't bad enough already, Mabel and I

are now scrubbed to within an inch of our lives.

And dressed in NEW DRESSES...
THAT MY MUM HAS CHOSEN.

Swish

Why?

A BRAND NEW FRILLY
PARTY DRESS –
YUCK!

Even Bertie has been
scrubbed up and is
wearing...
A BOW TIE?!

Velvety
trousers
too!

fidget
fidget

145

Just then Granny arrives (to help with vegetable chopping and to baby-sit). Otto is sitting on her shoulder, making her look like an OAP pirate.

"Why did you bring that winged menace here?" asks Dad with a groan.

"Oh, I couldn't leave him all alone," says Granny, stroking Otto as he hops onto her hand. "Besides, he'll keep me company while I baby-sit Bertie."

Dad gives Otto **A LOOK...**

"Well, just keep him away from the guests," warns Mum, before turning to me. "And don't think YOU can sneak off and play with Otto. In fact, here is a list of DOs and DON'Ts."

My mum hands me a list...

Mum wearing nail varnish: must be a special occasion!

Writing is on the other side

Party DOs

<u>Do</u> make <u>small talk</u> and pleasant chat
with all the guests

<u>Do</u> offer the guests snacks and drinks –
these are NOT for you

<u>Do</u> tell Mrs Musgrove that her hair looks
fabulous at every opportunity

<u>Do</u> laugh at <u>**all**</u> of Mr Musgrove's jokes,
especially the ones about golf

Party DON'Ts

<u>Don't</u> allow pets into the guest area

<u>Don't</u> be <u>RUDE</u> to Clarissa

<u>Don't</u> ~~EAT~~ anything tasty looking –
the best food is all for the guests

<u>Don't</u> have fun – this barbecue is
<u>NOT about fun</u>

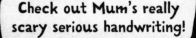

**Check out Mum's really
scary serious handwriting!**

Soon the guests start to arrive, including you-know-who...

ding! dong!

"Donny! So good to see you," grovels my dad, taking Mr Musgrove's coat. "You look well, doesn't he, Penny? He looks better than well..."

"He looks RIDICULOUSLY WELL," Mum beams.

"And as for you, Muriel..."

My mum has to stop to draw breath...

You look
UNBELIEVABLY,
FABULOUSLY,
AMAZING!

As Dad sweeps the Musgroves through to the barbecue,
my mum FORCES me to show Clarissa my room.

"Come along, darling," Mum says in a cheesy voice she
only puts on when she's trying too hard to be nice. "I'm
sure you two will be the
best of friends."

Cheesy
is my
department!

I know Mum is making me do this to help Dad impress his boss. I also want to help my dad. I'm going to have to dig deep, really deep to BE POLITE TO CLARISSA.

I plaster on my best
HAPPY GRIN.

"Yes, do come on up, Clarissa," I say through my grinning teeth. "I've got so much to show you..."

"Are you feeling alright?" asks Clarissa as we walk up the stairs to my room. (I'm not sure if she's falling for my plastered-on grin.)

"I'm fine," I declare. "So, I've got some er, board games we could play, or you could check out some books..." I say, desperately trying to keep my grin on. But Clarissa DOES NOT make it easy for me.

"Everything in your house is just so small," she says, pouting. She looks around my room with the expression you normally have when you look at your shoe and realise you've stepped in dog poo. "Small house, small room, small toys..."

Incredibly snooty look!

But she stops when she spots my pets.

"A mouse AND that repulsive class lizard," she screams.

"You've got them IN YOUR BEDROOM! They're

vermin! Isn't that, like, a health hazard?"

The grinning is hurting!

Beady eyes

"Well, you know, most pets are surprisingly clean," I

protest, but my mouth is now starting to hurt from all

the grinning.

"I particularly LOATHE that lizard," she scoffs. "If

Miss Primula thinks for one minute that I would look

after that disgusting...thing."

I imagine Edgar breaking out of his cage – angry and hell-bent on revenge on Clarissa.

As he jumps out of his cage he accidentally knocks over a jar of Plant Grow and he becomes HUGE!

He grabs Clarissa and takes her to the top of the house...

But as I imagine what a giant Edgar might do, something strange starts to happen – something I have never seen Edgar do before.

The real Edgar, my class lizard, looking happier than I have ever seen him, has escaped and is slinking up Clarissa's arm! If reptiles could purr or coo, that's what he'd be doing!

AAAAAAAAARRRRRGG

"I think he likes you," I say as I watch his tail swish round excitedly. "Correction – I think he **REALLY LIKES YOU!**"

But Clarissa has had enough and flees my room, wailing!

GGGGGGHHHHHHHHH!

Back at the barbecue, my dad is doing everything he can to impress Mr Musgrove.

Impressed (for some reason)

"Not only does this barbecue have some serious GRUNT," brags Dad. "But just wait until you see what I've got to cook on it..."

Dad claps his hands. This is my cue. I stagger out of the house, carrying an enormous tray full of FISH!

What is grunt?!?

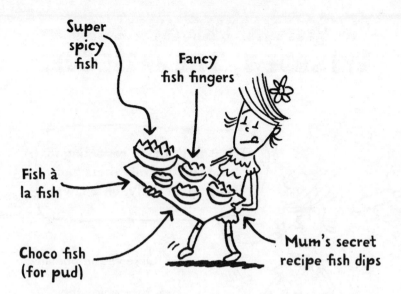

Super
spicy
fish

Fancy
fish fingers

Fish à
la fish

Choco fish
(for pud)

Mum's secret
recipe fish dips

As I bring out the platter of 'special fish' there is a round
of APPLAUSE.

Dad thanks the guests and waves to the crowd. Little
does he know that the barbecue is now MINUTES away
from DISASTER!

Let me explain what happened in the style of an over-
the-top documentary. As we discover what happens...

"WHEN NATURE ATTACKS – EPISODE 1, THE BARBECUE."

This is Beth Orsen reporting in a ridiculous frilly dress and standing, literally, on a lawn!

"Observe the humans as they enjoy their barbecue – little do they know they are about to be attacked. ATTACKED BY NATURE!"

"This man thinks he is about to serve the finest fresh fish. What he doesn't realise is that the fish have been mixed up with lizard food!"

"Live crickets are all over the guests, viciously

JUMPING ON THEM!"

"But this is just the START,

because it gets worse...for now

the menace is from above!"

Behold the
ominous shadow
in the sky!

"It's Granny's

PARROT OTTO!

He has escaped!

Observe as he PECKS

MRS MUSGROVE's GORGEOUS hair STYLE!"

"And look at this four-legged

TERROR – a common

house mouse...nibbling her

BEAUTIFULLY MANICURED TOES!"

"But this is all nothing when you

contemplate what is happening to

Clarissa Musgrove,

innocent, lovely Clarissa..."

"For she has A LIZARD perched on her

head – looking like he's in lizard heaven."

'HELP!'

screeches the child."

So fluffy and comfy!

"But there is no help...when

NATURE ATTACKS!"

I would love to tell you that was what happened, but sadly it was a lot less exciting than that. What REALLY happened when Dad skewered the fish was...

There was A STRANGE SMELL...

Dad's eyes watering from the smell!

The fish was OFF! It was rotten, past its sell-by-date –
IT STUNK!

The SMELL was SO BAD that people soon began making excuses to leave. And then my dad desperately put the fish on the barbecue and the smell got even worse!

Mr and Mrs Musgrove were the first to leave...

Mr Musgrove's golf trip with Dad was cancelled as they
left in a hurry...

And of course Clarissa couldn't resist a last smug remark
as she handed Edgar back to me.

STANK you very much! It might be a little house, but it sure is a BIG smell!

Annoying little wave!

Suddenly there is NO ONE IN THE HOUSE. It's been a twenty-four carat MEGA DISASTER coated in CALAMITY SAUCE. I can see my parents need cheering up. And when my parents really need cheering up there is one medicine that always works, a source of joy that can't be beaten...

"I'll order pizza," says Mum, smiling properly for the first time in ages.

"I was so close to getting a golf game with Mr Musgrove," sighs Dad, as we sit at the kitchen table.

"Did you see Mrs Musgrove's hair?" chuckles Mum, tucking into her pizza.

Scribbles loves the sprinkles

"If it was any bigger it would have its own airport..." cackles Granny. The whole family has cheered up.

So there is a (almost) happy ending and we even get ice cream for pudding.

A few days later and the BARBECUE DISASTER is now a distant memory – well, for me, anyway.

Cordy is visiting and we are CHATTING and PLOTTING...

We are putting together a cunning plan – a plan so ingenious that boffins in the future will one day talk about it at Cunning Plan College...

"OK, so run through the plan again," says Cordy as she takes a big slurp on the strawberry milkshake my mum has given us.

Yum!

The first part of the plan involves:

((a)) Planting my dad's rotten fish in Clarissa's expensive school bag.

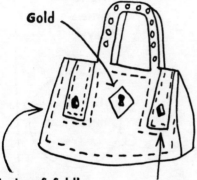

Gold

Lots of fiddly Italian hand stitching!

Rubies

Stinky fish that must have been dead for a million years!!!!

My dad still hasn't thrown the rotten fish out but intends to take them back to the shop to COMPLAIN about it in that annoying way that parents do.

The other part of the plan:

(b) Is how to get out of next year's family barbecue.

Tricky, as I live with my family and don't plan to move out for at least another eight years. Also it doesn't seem to matter how bad my parents' barbecues get, a year later the memory of the HORROR will have blurred and they'll think they are a good idea again.

The final part of the plan is the most ambitious:

(c) Finding a cheap way to send the Musgroves into space.

Again, sounds easy – hire a space ship, persuade the Musgroves to get on board and BLAST OFF! But it's actually quite complicated. According to my calculations, we need at least eight trillion pounds. And Clarissa doesn't believe anything I say...

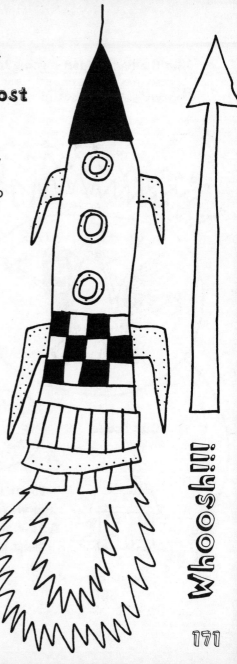

Whoosh!!

But the hardest part is going to be

COMBINING ALL OF THESE

Me and Cordy celebrating BIG TIME!

Our house

Edgar looking sad and waving goodbye. A few crickets might help him forget!

BBQ

173

Fortunately, when our plans gets too complicated Cordy

has got something SUPER EXCITING TO SHOW ME.

"I can't wait a second longer," she squeals, holding up

TICKETS TO THE DUSK LIFE MOVIE!

"We're going to the opening night! I had to unleash an

army of slavering zombie-pigs to get them!"

"Cordy!" I shriek.

"OK, my mum got them, she had to had to sit up until

2 o'clock in the morning to get them on the Dusk Light

website," says Cordy.

I can hardly sleep that night I am so excited. But the next day I'm quite sad because I have to take Edgar back to school.

I think Scribbles was pleased to get his room back.

"Well done, Beth," says Miss Primula, "Edgar looks in fine health – you've done a great job... Now I wonder who should look after him next."

"How about...Clarissa?" I suggest.
Clarissa gives me an EVIL STARE but sadly Miss Primula isn't listening.

Because the class has to go to the big hall straight away for another SPECIAL ASSEMBLY... to announce the winners of the model animal competition!

Giles Goddard is back at school...this time he has brought terrifying...

STICK INSECTS with him...

"Look at these creatures – they look...like STICKS!" observes the wildlife expert.

"Ooooh!" goes the whole hall. Although they are not very scary they are certainly quite creepy.

Oooooooo0OOooo0ooo0OOooooOoooOoooooO

As the applause dies down, Ms Hailey buzzes on to the stage – not literally, although she *is* dressed as a fly.

The room is totally silent as Mr Goddard opens an envelope...

"We travelled the length and breadth of the country," states Mr Goddard. "But one class stood out above all the others...

"And the winning class is..." (I could feel THE WHOLE SCHOOL HOLDING ITS BREATH) **"Miss Primula's!"**

OMG!!!

oOOOOOoooooooOhHHHHhhhHHHHHHhhHh!

Our class will be going to the safari park! This is
GREAT NEWS...

Of course Clarissa has to
boast that she has been
there LOADS OF TIMES
– AND she thinks she
should get special credit.

"If it wasn't for my giraffe, we would never have won,"
she brags. (Although I'm pretty sure I overheard Ms
Hailey saying to Mr Mavers to "stash that PAPIER-
MÂCHÉ MONSTROSITY behind the bicycle sheds".)

Back in our classroom, Miss Primula can hardly contain herself...

"This really is super, super news!" she says, giving Edgar a couple of extra crickets as a super, super treat.

Happy Miss Primula!

Happy Edgar!

Not so happy cricket!

The only problem with GREAT news is that we all find it really hard to concentrate for the rest of the day...

My trying-to-really-really concentrate face!

You know it's a **BIG** day when you wake up so early that it is PITCH DARK OUTSIDE.

But today is the day of the visit to the SAFARI PARK and there is ABSOLUTELY NO WAY I am going to oversleep.

On days like this I wish that instead of an alarm clock I had an angry goblin who lived in my sock drawer who would shout at me to WAKE UP!

But for now I have to rely on my old alarm clock. I'm so
excited that I bound out of bed straight away.

I'm sorry,
Scribbles,
but there
are **NO PETS
ALLOWED**
on the trip.

Hmph!

Fortunately, Scribbles is an
understanding kind of mouse
and doesn't seem too bothered
– especially when I give him
EXTRA CHEESY toast for
his breakfast.

All is
forgiven!

For once I can't hear my dad singing. But downstairs

there's something worse. An almighty...

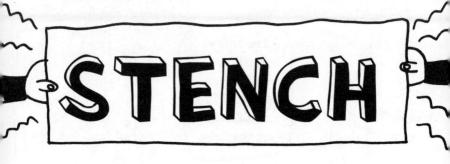

"These bad boys are going
back to the fishmongers
TODAY," says Dad.

Can you believe it? The barbecue

was ages ago and my dad STILL wants to

take the rotting fish BACK to the fishmongers?!

It's a mad idea – and probably a health hazard – but it's

SO Dad...

"See, I told you these briefcases were a top acquisition," says my dad as he rams all the rotting fish fingers into one of them.

Inside the bag!

I'm once again reminded that I STILL need a new school bag.

Unfortunately all of this messing around means Dad has made me LATE FOR THE TRIP.

There is only one solution – Dad has to drop me off in the car on his way to the fishmongers.
I tell Dad to get to school as quickly as possible.

We're going by coach and the coach is one of the most exciting parts of any school trip - AND IT'S ALL ABOUT WHERE YOU SIT.

Beth's quick guide to where to sit on a coach:

Driver goes here

FRONT OF THE BUS

Unless you want to spend the trip talking to the teachers, this area is to be avoided.

I get to school just as the bell rings and
my class are about to get on the coach.

I was starting
to think perhaps
you'd been whisked
away in the night
by ghouls...

Everyone is **SUPER EXCITED** as we wait to
get onboard and I don't have time to tell Cordy about
my dad's fishy briefcase.

Miss Primula sits up at the front and behind her there is a MAD SCRAMBLE for seats...it's all elbows and shoving. Cordy and I decide not to get involved.

Unsurprisingly Clarissa and her friends are hogging the back seat.

Desiree Fogle

Josh Wyndham

"It's soooo cool back here," gloats Clarissa. "We can EAT AND MUCK ABOUT!"

Unfortunately for Clarissa, Miss Primula hears her and in her MOST TERRIFYING VOICE tells them, "There will be no eating or mucking about on this trip!"

We are soon there, and waiting to meet us is Giles Goddard himself.

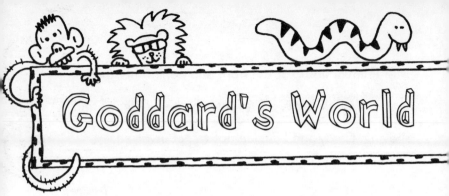

Goddard's World

"WELCOME TO GODDARD'S WORLD OF WONDERBEASTS!" He beams. "And trust me, on this tour there will be NO dwarf hamsters, NO tiny guinea pigs and NO toothless snails. Because this is the REAL DEAL! This is a safari park with big and scary wildlife!"

Mr Goddard is in his element and it's all about getting 'hands on' with tigers and 'up close and personal' with hippos...
WE CAN'T WAIT!

hair done specially

orange high-tech shades

# of Wonderbeasts

We are all led onto one of the safari park's minibuses, which are reinforced with protective grills and toughened front bumpers. Giles Goddard himself is driving and giving us the tour.

"OK, settle down, everyone," he crackles through the bus tannoy system. "There are some pretty wild wonderbeasts out there. Like all wildlife, if you treat them with respect you'll have no problem. So windows shut, hands inside the bus at all times..."

It all sounds really EXCITING and we are completely silent. Apart from Clarissa...

As soon as we get going we start to see some amazing wildlife. Mr Goddard drives us through a series of huge enclosures where the animals roam about wherever they want – with no cages! Everyone's faces are pressed to the windows as we spot lions and tigers in the first area, but as soon as we drive into the monkey enclosure Clarissa opens her window...

"These hairy guys are really quite harmless," she sneers. But then a **BABOON** grabs her lunch...

Panic
panic

Hairy
monkey
arm

Window down:
oops!

Fancy
bon-bons

Very dainty
sandwich

"Stop the bus!" she cries. "Do you have any idea how expensive that baguette was?"

We, of course, find this HILARIOUS and even Giles Goddard has a chuckle – but he refuses to stop the bus.

I begin to wonder what the baboons will do with Clarissa's fancy sandwiches. In fact, what do the animals do when the safari park is closed?

Please do partake, my hairy friend.

Maybe the baboons run a small business selling the stuff they steal from silly visitors.

The lions probably operate a multiplex cinema in a hidden bunker under their enclosure.

The penguins OBVIOUSLY have an ice skating rink in the back of their space where they charge the other animals to skate.

And the giraffes probably run a crèche for all the baby animals.

But before I can find out if the lions really do run a cinema, the driving part of the visit is over.

"Everyone off!" says Mr Goddard. "And bring your lunches – if you haven't fed them to the monkeys..."

We all climb off the bus, taking our bags with us.

I'm disappointed, not one mention of a vampire bat.

"I need first aid!" wails Clarissa. "That monkey touched me!" She's doing what sounds to everyone (apart from Miss Primula) like fake crying. To underline her point she is holding her arm straight out in front of her and waggling her wrist.

Lip going wobbly

Terrible injury

Once Miss Primula has taken Clarissa to have her hands washed, we continue off around the safari park.

Next the World of Wonderbeasts tour goes to the

REPTILE ZONE

We enter a doorway into a large, warm and slightly

dark area. There are floor to ceiling vivariums all around

us – Edgar would love it! – and in the centre is a large

crocodile pool.

The pool has a fence running right round it – but we

can see some crocs swimming in the water!

"Is it me or is there a slightly strange smell in here?"
Cordy wonders out loud as she sniffs the air.

Strange
smell

And it's
NOT
cheese

"I think you're just a bit sensitive to
animals," I reply. Although I think I can
smell something strange too.

"OK, I need a volunteer!" pipes up Giles Goddard as
we try to work out where the smell is coming from.

Before we even know what he wants a volunteer for,
EVERYONE'S HAND GOES UP.

"This lucky volunteer will get to PET the newest

addition to our reptilian family — a baby croc!"

he announces proudly.

Quite a few hands GO DOWN (but not mine).

My hand is
still up

Miss Primula gets to decide and all of us who want to do it give her our best 'pick me' puppy dog eyes. But Miss Primula has already made up her mind...

"As a reward for looking after Edgar so well," says Miss Primula, **"I choose...Beth!"**

I am excited and nervous as Giles Goddard prepares for us to ENTER THE JAWS OF DEATH.

OK, maybe that's a bit of an exaggeration, but we are actually going in with the crocodiles!

First of all he unlocks the gate and we walk INTO the enclosure. That bit is FINE but he then SHUTS THE DOOR BEHIND US.

Then we walk a few stairs down to the side of the crocodile pool.

"Well done, Beth, you're keeping nice and calm," Mr Goddard whispers.

The path leads to a small island where the littlest crocodile of all is basking on a rock. We slowly approach and under close supervision...

I am now ACTUALLY STROKING A CROCODILE!

Yes, I am a bit tense!

But Mr Goddard seems concerned by something.

"What *is* that smell?" he says.

In fact, the smell is so bad I need to cover my nose.

Cordy, who can see I'm suffering, throws me something.

"My swamp monster mask!"
she shouts. "Put it on!"

But even with the mask over my nose the
SMELL is getting **WORSE AND WORSE!**

And the bigger crocodiles, the ones swimming in the pool, who had been ignoring us up until now, seem to be getting excited by it!

"Stay calm," says Mr Goddard, "We seem to have a small crocodile issue... It's really nothing to worry about. You wait here, I'm going to get a stick – just as a safety precaution."

It's only now that I realise the source of the problem – the smell is coming from...

MY BRIEFCASE!

Well, not MY briefcase – DAD'S BRIEFCASE – I must

have picked up the wrong one this morning!

AND IT'S FULL OF ROTTEN FISH FINGERS!

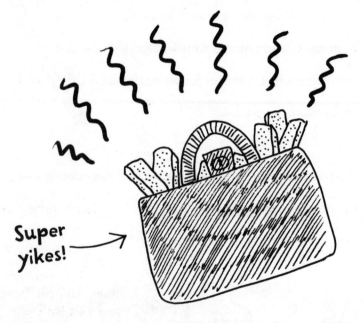

Super
yikes!

DISASTER!

The bigger crocodiles are now closing in on the island and Mr Goddard and his 'safety stick' are on the other side of the enclosure!

"Don't panic, Beth!" he shouts. "I'll get a rope!"

Fortunately I'm not the panicky type because sticks and ropes and crocodiles are a combination that would make most people PANIC!

As the crocodiles get closer, I can't help wondering what happened to *my* briefcase. Dad must have been quite embarrassed in the fishmongers...

So, I'm surrounded by crocodiles, I've got a briefcase
full of fish fingers, I'm wearing a swamp monster mask...
AND MISS PRIMULA IS ABOUT TO CALL MY
PARENTS!

Oh yes, Miss Primula is now on the phone to my dad –
it's officially an EMERGENCY!

So now you know how I got here, I guess you'll be
wanting to know how I get out?

While Giles Goddard tries to lasso me with a rope, I start to think.

I am armed with TWO things:

FIRSTLY

The briefcase full of stinky fish fingers

SECONDLY

Knowledge

Holding my breath behind the swamp-monster mask, I open the briefcase and I throw it into the water.

Just as I'd hoped, most of the crocodiles quickly start munching on all the lovely old fish (a couple of them even take a chunk out of the briefcase – I've never seen a crocodile's eyes water before!).

The stinky fish are going to save me! I have a tiny window of time before they finish eating, and I make my way CAREFULLY towards the exit...

But as I am about to climb free I am faced by a **VERY LARGE CROC**. On to the KNOWLEDGE.

I remember the trip to Pet Mega Store and what they told us about reptiles.

I was hoping I wouldn't have to do it, but very slowly and carefully I reach down and TICKLE the crocodile under the chin...

Just in time, Mr Goddard's lasso lands on me. With some fellow zookeepers helping him, he pulls me up and out of the enclosure!

The crowd CHEERS AND APPLAUDS as I step out to safety.

Tickle

tickle tickle

"What a relief!" gasps Miss Primula.

For a minute I thought Miss Primula was going to blub!

"I would have been out in half the time," scoffs Clarissa, although she soon pipes down when Cordy reminds her she barely survived an encounter with a peckish baboon.

After our packed lunches (Giles Goddard gives me a free lunch from the Wonderbeast Café), the trip is over.

"Thanks for coming," says Mr Goddard waving us off. "And if you want a job as a reptile keeper, Beth..."

On the trip back, ME AND CORDY get to sit on the
back seat of the bus!

"The crocodile tamer should get the best seat," says
Miss Primula, proudly. "But you won't be alone..."

Joining us at the back of the bus is a familiar figure...
MY DAD!

"I took a taxi here when I got the call
from Miss Primula," Dad pants.
"Thank goodness you're safe. Now
who wants to sing some **happy driving tunes?**"

A few days later and I have now put the incident at the safari park firmly BEHIND ME.

Even though I really like Edgar, I think I am going to avoid reptiles for a while.

In fact, something really exciting is about to happen because today is the day ME AND CORDY GO TO THE CINEMA...

And we are

BEYOND EXCITED!

That's an understatement!

We're going to see the latest Dusk Light film. We're on our way to the cinema when my mum decides to tell us something.

Weird face!

"I've got a secret that I must share with you, girls," she whispers as she drives us to the cinema. "I've had a crush on Bobby Gothick for the longest time."

That is officially MORE ICKY than feeding Edgar live crickets, but it's worse when Mum REPEATS THIS **LOUDLY** IN THE QUEUE.

But things are about to get a whole lot worse... What could be the worst **POSSIBLE** thing to spot in the cinema queue?

An alien with body-hygiene issues? No.

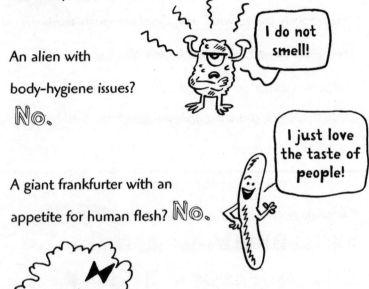

I do not smell!

I just love the taste of people!

A giant frankfurter with an appetite for human flesh? No.

Sparkly

sparkly

sparkly

Clarissa Musgrove?

Oh yes!

And there she is in her 'going out' outfit, all sparkly and red carpet–y.

Because my mum is there, Cordy and I have to make 'polite conversation'.

"How lovely to see you," says Cordy through teeth so gritted she sounds like a ventriloquist's dummy.

"I didn't know you were a Dusk Light fan," I add, trying to lighten the mood.

"Teenage werewolves?" sneers Clarissa. "They're lamer than a hamster with three legs. But my dad knows the director, so we've got a private **VIP** room..."

Smugger than smug

Painful grinning

I hadn't even noticed
Mr Musgrove was there
as he was carrying a box
of popcorn SO

HUGE

he was completely
hidden by it.

Fortunately they enter
their private VIP room
and the door shuts.

"She is SUCH a lovely girl,"
says my mum in a cheery
voice. But we all know
she doesn't really mean it.

Mr Musgrove →

We can **FINALLY** watch the film, and as predicted it is AWESOME... Here is what happens in 3 boxes:

Brad and Kim
are at SUMMER CAMP
by a lake...

When a SWAMP MONSTER
emerges from the lake on the FULL
MOON the teenage werewolves
must save the camp...

Only DeShaun (played by Bobby
Gothick in SUPER SWOON
MODE) can defeat the
monster...

When the lights go up we are in for a BIG treat –

BOBBY GOTHICK IS LIVE AND IN THE BUILDING!!!!!!!!!

I have **NEVER EVER** seen Cordy looking this **soppy!**

And as for Mum...

"I think I'm in love," says Cordy.

Let me out! I'm a VIP!

bang

bang

"I *am* in love," squeals Mum.

(But as we clap and go wild, spare a thought for Clarissa – we discovered later that she got locked in her VIP room as Bobby Gothick made his surprise visit, and DIDN'T SEE HIM AT ALL...)

"Hello, Dusk Light fans," says Bobby, dazzling us with his laser-beam smile. He waves. The crowd go wild.
He waves again. The crowd goes WILDER! But there is more!

"I have gifts for everyone!" he says in that very cool Bobby Gothick way. He then flicks up a hand and does the 'werewolf claw thing' he does in the films.

MY MOUTH FALLS OPEN.

Cordy gasps.

MUM NEARLY FAINTS.

He then presents us all with a
FREEBIE – it's the latest Dusk Light
merchandise – a brand-new
Dusk Light bag!

I am sooo
happy!!!

THE END

If you liked this adventure, you won't believe what happens to me next time... Turn over for a sneak peek!

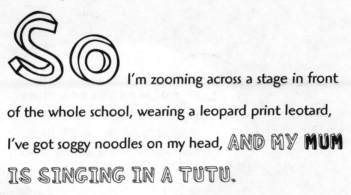

So I'm zooming across a stage in front of the whole school, wearing a leopard print leotard, I've got soggy noodles on my head, AND MY **MUM** IS SINGING IN A TUTU.

How did I get here? Let's go back to the beginning...

Read

BADLY DRAWN BETH:
The Show Must Go On!

to find out what happens next!